Madeline Pearl

The Peacock Tree

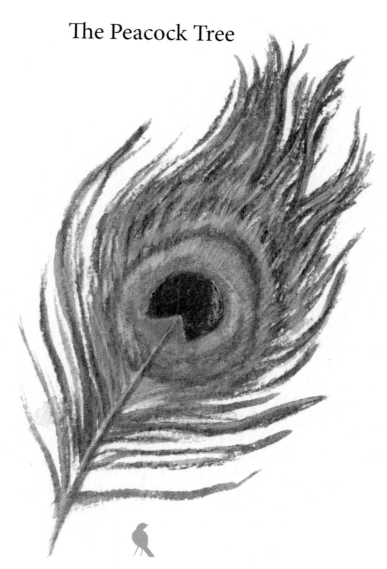

Nightingale Books

A CIP catalogue record for this title is
available from the British Library.

ISBN 978-1-83875-766-3

Nightingale Books is an imprint of
Pegasus Elliot MacKenzie Publishers Ltd.
www.pegasuspublishers.com

First Published in 2024

Nightingale Books
Sheraton House Castle Park
Cambridge England

Printed & Bound in Great Britain

Dedication

To the peacocks and the children
of Woodcroft Castle…

An hour's train from London
in the parish of Etton on the grounds
of Woodcroft Castle
stands a tree all the children know…
The Peacock Tree.

The Peacock Tree is proud and tall and full of branches. Five children holding hands cannot circle it.

But six can.

Each night, the peahens fly from the castle tower
to the high branches of the Peacock Tree.
The peacocks join them, crossing the moat and
fluttering across the field to the low branches.

The sun sets on the Peacock Tree.
The stars rise.
The peacocks sleep.

At night the Castle and the Peacock Tree whisper.
When the children sleep and all is quiet, they
whisper of olden days when the Peacock Tree
was just a sapling...

The Castle told the Peacock Sapling of the men
and women who built the Castle stone by stone,
of how they needed deep moats and many swords.
But the Peacock Sapling did not listen to the Castle.

The Castle told the Peacock Sapling of the knights who would gather under heavy armor on black horses and do battle on the grounds on

But the Peacock Sapling did
not listen to the Castle.

The Castle told the Peacock Sapling that someday it would be six children wide. Now, the Peacock Tree listens to the Castle.

Together, they remember when there were no trains or cars or planes. When there was only sun and night and wrong and right.

Together, they whisper to the saplings in the forest and the roses in the garden, about the simpler times of a simpler place which were not always better.

The sun rises early and so do the peacocks.
They wait by the crumbly well.
The one with the wooden bucket with no bottom.

They wait on the windowsills.
They wait on the benches.
They wait for the children of the Castle.

The peacocks caw.
The peacocks wail.
The children awake.

Down the creaky stairs, the children
race to the garden.

The peacocks peck and feast.

When the seed is gone and the peacocks fed,
the children look up at the Peacock Tree.
They see it proud and tall and full of branches.

They begin to climb.

The Castle whispers to the
Peacock Tree,
"Take care of my children."

The Peacock
Tree listens.

The Peacock Tree whispers to the children,
"Take care of my peacocks."

The children listen.

About the Author

My name is Madeline Pearl, and I am publishing this book at the ripe old age of 17. This is my first book, although I've been drawing since I could speak.
I live in Princeton and attend Princeton Day School. I am a daughter, a sister, a friend, a student, and a lover of castles and peacocks! I owe so much to the happenstance of a supportive community, and in ever-widening communities, I hope to continue to grow as an artist and as a human being.

Acknowledgements

Thank you most of all to Spencer and Emily for not only having a magical castle, with such peacocks and such a tree, but for letting my family stay in it so generously! Thanks to my mom and dad for praising my scribbles. Thank you to my grandmas, sister, brother, aunts, uncles, cousins, family, friends, and teachers for helping me to understand, like the children at the end of this book, how we must all support each other. To my mentor, my support-system, and my weekly inspiration–Barbara DiLorenzo–I realize a simple, heartfelt "thank you!" is not enough.